For Fatima and Iain - J C

LITTLE TIGER PRESS LTD,
an imprint of the Little Tiger Group
1 Coda Studios, 189 Munster Road, London SW6 6AW
Imported into the EEA by Penguin Random House Ireland,
Morrison Chambers, 32 Nassau Street, Dublin D02 YH68
www.littletiger.co.uk

First published in Great Britain 2023

Text and illustrations copyright © Jane Chapman 2023
Visit Jane Chapman at www.janekchapman.com
Jane Chapman has asserted her right to be identified as
the author and illustrator of this work under the Copyright,
Designs and Patents Act, 1988

A CIP catalogue record for this book is available from
the British Library

Printed in China
LTP/2800/4871/0922

10 9 8 7 6 5 4 3 2 1

FSC
www.fsc.org
MIX
Paper from
responsible sources
FSC® C017606

The Forest Stewardship Council® (FSC®) is an international, non-governmental
organisation dedicated to promoting responsible management of the world's
forests. FSC® operates a system of forest certification and product labelling
that allows consumers to identify wood and wood-based products from well-
managed forests.

For more information about the FSC®, please visit their website at www.fsc.org

WPK
2123

Mole's
Quiet
PLACE

JANE CHAPMAN

LITTLE TIGER

LONDON

The moonlit forest was silent.

Beaver and Mole gazed out of their treehouse
at the starry sky.

"I look forward to this time together each day," Mole smiled.
"Me too," agreed Beaver, as he lit the lanterns, just like
their old friend Bear had done.

Silvered leaves turned
gold in the lantern's light.

"The beam makes a path over the woods and across the lake," exclaimed Beaver. "Our treehouse is a lighthouse!"

Mole laughed. "So we'll always find our way home!"

Floorboards creaked as there was a knock on the door.

"I saw the light so I knew you were here!"
beamed Rabbit. "And Bunny wondered
if there was any cake?"
"Come and sit next to me," offered Mole.
"Beaver is reading me a story."

Everyone laughed loudly at the funny bits and
their giggles floated out across the treetops.

They were settling down for story
time the next night when Squirrel's
whiskers appeared.

"I heard you chatting and wondered
whether you'd like a song?"

Mole shuffled over to make
space for the ukulele.
Then Mouse climbed in.
"I thought I smelled
something delicious!"

From then on, it seemed to Mole that every
evening brought more and more visitors.

hilly out there.
come in?"

"It's a bit busy, Beaver," Mole whispered, one blustery night.

"Yes, it's lovely that we have space for so many," Beaver smiled.

"Our port in a storm!" squeaked Mouse, shaking off the rain. "I brought some company, because I knew you wouldn't mind."

"There's room for us all," laughed Beaver. "Right, Mole?"

But Mole wasn't there.
   "She said she was going to follow the light down to the lake," Rabbit explained.

Beaver took Bear's big umbrella from
its place by the door and went hunting
for his friend in the dark.

"Mole!

Mole!"

"I'm here."

Mole was wrapped up warm
against the weather.

Beaver sat beside her, "What's up, my friend?"

Mole sighed. "I love the excitement our visitors bring, but I miss our peaceful evenings. The space helped me rest and think."

"I understand," Beaver smiled. "We all need a safe place to call our own."

The rain pattering on the lake gave Beaver an idea.

The next day, the treehouse gang
began a new project just for Mole.
There was sawing and hammering,
painting and stitching until . . .

"It should be the perfect size for a mole,"
announced Beaver when he revealed the surprise.

Mole didn't know
what to say.
"For me?" she stuttered.
"That's so kind,
thank you!"

Her friends waved merrily as Mole
rowed away from the shore.

In the middle of the lake Mole felt perfectly at peace.
The boat rocked to the rhythm of the waves.
Dragonflies zipped in and out of bullrushes.

Mole felt the warmth of the sun
and breathed deeply,
while the
afternoon drifted
silently into evening.

Tiny stars emerged in the dusky sky when
a beam of light shone out above the forest.

"Oh, Beaver has lit
the lanterns!" Mole laughed.

She could see why all her friends were
attracted to the welcoming glow.

"Me too," smiled Mole, as she
turned her boat around.

From then on, every day, when
she had finished her quiet time,
Mole followed the light back to shore.

Back to her treehouse, and the
loving warmth of the friends she
knew she would always find there.